P9-CDZ-332

Bevan is a very, very old bear.

His fur is a little patchy and his paws are rather scrappy, but he still smiles.

When Bevan was a brand-new bear, he lived in a
large nursery with three children and Nanny.

The children had lots and lots of wonderful toys,
and Bevan joined in all their games.

The grandchild became a young woman. She met a
young man and they got married. Her husband whisked
her off to live on his parents' ranch. Bevan went too.

Soon they had a child who loved Bevan.
Bevan and the little boy would share a
saddle and ride the trails.

After years of saving their wages, the boy and his friend bought a colorful bus and took off. Bevan went too.

The baby grew into a brave girl and left home for camp. Bevan went too.

Camp was an adventure. The little girl's head was full of boats and games, flashlight tales, and all her new friends. Bevan fell down the side of her bed and was forgotten.

When camp was over, the little girl packed up her bag and left for home . . . without Bevan. Children came to the cabin, and they went again. Bevan stayed lost, under the bed with the dried leaves blown in from the woods.

At last Bevan was discovered by a cleaner. He took him and sat him on a shelf in the Lost and Found. Dust grew thick on his fur. But nobody came to claim him.

His fur is a little patchy and his paws are
rather scrappy, but he still smiles.

And I love him very, very, very much!

For little Billy

Text Copyright and Illustration Copyright © 2021 Petra Brown
Design Copyright © 2021 Sleeping Bear Press

All rights reserved. No part of this book may be reproduced in any manner
without the express written consent of the publisher, except in the case of brief
excerpts in critical reviews and articles. All inquiries should be addressed to:

SLEEPING BEAR PRESS™

2395 South Huron Parkway, Suite 200
Ann Arbor, MI 48104
www.sleepingbearpress.com

Printed and bound in the United States.

10 9 8 7 6 5 4 3 2 1

Library of Congress Cataloging-in-Publication Data

Names: Brown, Petra, author. | Brown, Petra, illustrator.
Title: Bevan / written and illustrated by Petra Brown.
Description: Ann Arbor, Michigan : Sleeping Bear Press, [2021] |
Audience: Ages 4-8. | Summary: Over many years a teddy bear named
Bevan enters the   lives of different boys and girls, and after countless
adventures Bevan   is old and patchy, but still loved.
Identifiers: LCCN 2021010657 | ISBN 9781534111103 (hardcover)
Subjects: CYAC: Teddy bears—Fiction. | Love—Fiction.
Classification: LCC PZ7.B816683 Be 2021 | DDC [E]—dc23
LC record available at https://lccn.loc.gov/2021010657

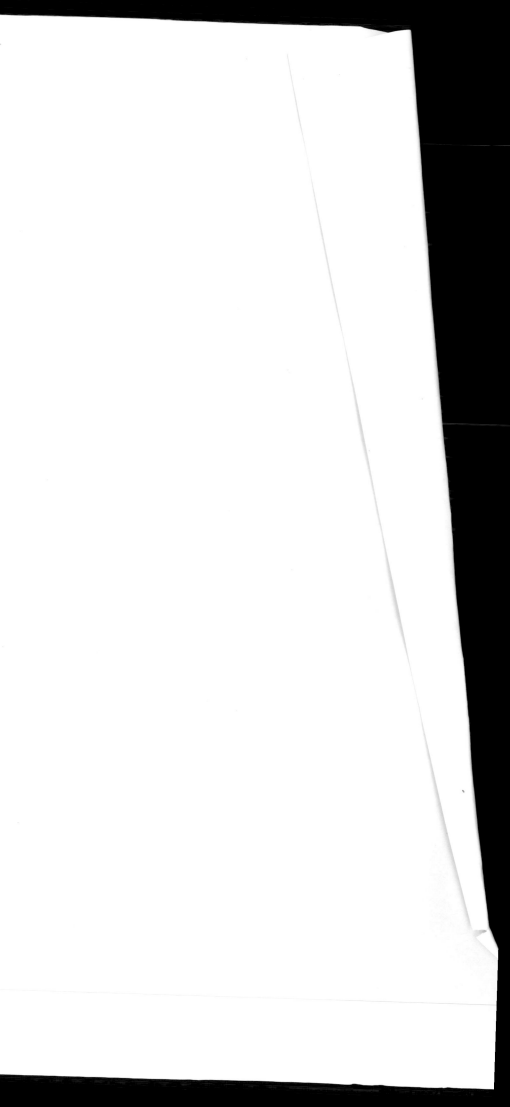